ANIMAL TALES FROM THE BIBLE

A storm had blown up out of nowhere. The wind howled and the sea boiled and foamed. A ship appeared and the whale could hear anguished cries from those on board.

The whale swam closer... suddenly he gulped and swallowed. He could feel something large travelling down his throat and into his stomach. Something large and totally indigestible. Whatever could it be?

The whale isn't the only animal who's in for a big surprise. Mrs Noah's cat finds she's not in charge of the ark, and Balaam's donkey comes face to face with an angel! Avril Rowlands retells ten Old Testament tales with her trademark humour and originality.

AVRIL ROWLANDS is the author of many books for children, including the very popular *Tales from the Ark* and its sequels, and *The Animals' Christmas* and *The Animals' Easter*. Among Avril's hobbies are swimming, walking, theatre and steam railways.

For Dormouse

Animal Tales from the Bible

Avril Rowlands
Illustrations by Rosslyn Moran

LION
Children's Books

Published by
Lion Publishing plc
Sandy Lane West, Oxford, England
www.lion-publishing.co.uk
ISBN 0 7459 4458 2

First edition 2001
10 9 8 7 6 5 4 3 2 1

A catalogue record for this book is available
from the British Library

Typeset in 12/16 ZapfCalligraphic
Printed and bound in Great Britain by
Omnia Books Ltd, Glasgow

CONTENTS

To Begin...

If someone asks you about animals in the Bible, what is the first story you think of? It might be Noah's ark, or the whale that swallowed Jonah. In fact, there are many animal tales in the Bible. Some animals have a big part to play, like Balaam's donkey, while others are referred to only in passing. And many more animals, insects and birds that are not mentioned must have witnessed biblical events.

Inspired by the writings of the Old Testament, this book contains stories about all kinds of animals. In many cases I've allowed my imagination to run free, thinking 'what if...' rather than following the Bible text too closely. Each story is different, but all of them show something of the way in which God works in the world, and of his love and care for every living thing.

1

The Snake in the Garden

*When God created the world, he made a beautiful garden—
the Garden of Eden—and filled it with plants and animals,
insects and birds. He created man and woman, and put
them in the garden so that they might look after everything
in it. Everyone was happy there, except for the snake…*

The snake was bored. None of the other animals
understood why.

'Bored?' said the lion. 'You can't possibly be bored
in the Garden of Eden. Why, it's… it's…'

'Paradise,' squeaked the mouse.

'Precisely,' said the lion.

And it was paradise. The world had just been
made by God and everything was new, sparkling and
very beautiful. It was never too hot and never too
cold, and although it did rain at times, they were

refreshing showers, never too little, never too much. Flowers bloomed all year long, a riot of shapes and colours, and their scent filled the air.

Animals, insects and birds lived together with never a cross word between them. Some were handsome, some were ugly, and some were very odd indeed, but they had all been made by God, and he loved every one. And Adam and Eve—the man and the woman God had created to look after them—filled the days with laughter.

'How on earth can you be bored?' asked the hyena.

'There's nothing to do,' said the snake.

'There's plenty to do!' cried the wolf. 'I could never get tired of being here.'

'God visits us every day,' said the ox. 'He's never boring. What more do you want?'

'I don't know,' said the snake in a sulky voice.

'Why don't you speak to God?' asked the rabbit. 'I'm sure he'd come up with something. I've always found God very approachable.'

The snake said nothing and slipped away. He did not like the animals worrying about him. Why should they? He never worried about them. They were dull, like the garden. Dull and boring.

The snake moved restlessly through the lush grass, past amazing plants and trees, and fabulously bright flowers. He saw nothing of the beauty that surrounded him. Should he speak to God, he wondered? He always knew when God was there. He would see the trailing edge of his gleaming shadow and hear his laughter on the evening air as he talked with Adam and Eve. Other animals, insects and birds would flock to meet him, but the snake seldom joined them.

He wandered deeper and deeper until he found himself in a clearing right at the very heart of the garden. In front of him stood two fine trees, taller than the rest. One was the Tree of Life and the other the Tree of Knowledge of Good and Evil. The snake scarcely glanced at the Tree of Life, but stood staring at the Tree of Knowledge of Good and Evil, gazing at it as if he was seeing it for the first time.

There were thousands of trees in the Garden of Eden, but the Tree of Knowledge of Good and Evil was different. Its branches rose proudly, high into the air, as if they would reach heaven. Its leaves were glossily green and it was laden with glowing fruit. The snake licked his lips and moved closer.

'It's forbidden you know,' said a voice.

He turned to find Adam and Eve and some of the animals.

'What's forbidden?' asked the snake.

'To eat the fruit of that tree. God has told us not to eat it.'

'Why?'

'I don't know,' said Adam.

'There must be a good reason,' said Eve. But she sounded unsure and her eyes, like the snake's, were fixed on the golden fruit.

'It doesn't make sense,' grumbled the snake. 'Why did God put the tree here in the first place, if he doesn't want us to eat its fruit?'

'Perhaps it's some sort of test?' suggested the lion.

'Perhaps it was some sort of mistake,' said the rabbit.

'God doesn't make mistakes,' said the fox.

'Maybe not, but if it was a mistake, couldn't God uncreate it?' asked the nightingale, flying in and out of the tree's branches.

'But I've just said that God doesn't make mistakes,' the fox repeated patiently.

The humans and animals left the clearing and the snake followed, smiling to himself. Life in the garden had suddenly become interesting. The snake had a plan.

It was a simple plan. The snake was short, and the fruit too high for him to reach. If he could persuade Eve to pluck one of the fruit, he could take it from her. Even if she ate some of it she might give the rest to him. For the snake guessed that she, like himself, longed to eat the fruit.

The snake was no longer bored.

If I could eat just a few pips, it would be enough, he thought. Enough for me to have knowledge.

Enough for me to be like God.

So the snake followed Eve and began to whisper in her ear.

'How beautiful the fruit looks. Golden and glowing.'

Eve sighed.

'How exciting to eat something we've never tasted, something ripe and juicy,' the snake went on.

Eve said nothing.

'Don't you think it's unfair of God to put such a beautiful thing in our garden and then forbid us to eat it? After all, what harm can it do?'

'Perhaps God likes to eat it himself,' Eve said doubtfully. 'And it's not our garden. It's God's garden.'

'But he made it for us and he put you and Adam in charge,' said the snake slyly. 'Besides, there's enough fruit for everyone—God, animals and humans.'

Then the snake left Eve to think about what he had said. The following day he found her in the clearing, gazing up at the tree.

'Just look at those branches, almost breaking under the weight,' said the snake. 'It's such a beautiful-looking tree. Wouldn't it be sad if the branches broke because no one picked the fruit?'

'It would,' said Eve.

'Anyway, God wouldn't notice if just one or two fruit were missing.'

Eve looked at the fruit with longing and the snake was satisfied.

For three days the snake followed Eve and whispered in her ear, trying to persuade her to pick the fruit of the Tree of Knowledge of Good and Evil.

'Just think how wonderful it would be to have knowledge,' he said. 'Wouldn't it be nice to know everything?'

'But we mustn't,' Eve replied. 'We mustn't even touch the fruit, let alone eat it. Otherwise we'll die. God said so.'

'Nonsense,' said the snake. 'God wouldn't want anything he'd created to die.'

'Why did God say it, then?'

'Perhaps it was to frighten you. After all, God knows that when you eat the fruit, you'll be like God and know what's good and what's evil.'

'I'd like that,' said Eve. She took a step towards the tree.

'Of course you would,' said the snake, licking his lips. He could almost taste the delicious fruit in his mouth and feel it melting on his tongue.

'God only said it to frighten you,' he repeated.

'Do you really think so?' Eve asked. She took another step towards the tree.

'Yes,' said the snake, following closely on her heels.

'Truly?'

Eve took a third step.

'Truly.'

'Very well then.'

She ran to the tree, stretched up her hand and picked one of the fruit. The snake's mouth watered. She bit deeply into it and the juice ran down her chin.

The snake licked his lips. Soon, he thought, soon. She'll spit out the pips and I'll be able to eat them. But

Eve ate every part of the fruit, pips and all, then reached up to pluck another.

'Might I,' asked the snake, 'possibly have a taste? Just one small nibble?'

Eve turned to him, a cold look in her eyes. The fruit had given her knowledge of good and evil, and she now saw the snake's plan.

'You?' she said mockingly. 'You only want to eat the fruit to cause mischief. You want to take over from God. If you think I'm going to give you any of it, you're mistaken!'

She ran to find Adam and between them they ate every last scrap.

That evening the snake hid when he saw the sunset splashing the sky with red, for he knew then that God was coming. Not that he was afraid to meet God, he told himself, for he had done nothing wrong. Not a bite from that fruit had passed his lips and he would say so, if he was asked. He felt God's shadow touch him and heard his voice, no longer laughing.

'Adam and Eve. Where are you?'

Adam and Eve slowly came out from behind a bush. They, too, had been hiding.

'Why are you hiding from me?' God asked.

Adam looked and Eve, and Eve looked at Adam, but neither of them spoke. Both of them were afraid.

'Did you eat the fruit that was forbidden?'

'Eve gave me some, so I ate it,' Adam said

uncomfortably. 'I can't say I was sure which tree it came from...' his voice trailed away.

'Why did you do this?' God asked Eve.

'The snake tricked me into it,' she said.

'It's very easy to blame others,' the snake hissed, coming out of hiding, but God wasn't listening.

'Now you know what is good and what is bad, you cannot stay in the Garden of Eden,' God said sadly.

'Why not?' asked Eve.

'When I created this garden, it was perfect. There was no stain of evil on it. I made it with love, and I gave you and Adam everything you could wish for. I also gave you freedom—the freedom to choose to obey me or disobey. In return I asked just one small thing. Not to eat the fruit of that tree. By eating it, you yourselves have brought wickedness into this garden. That is why you cannot stay. No one can stay. You will both have to leave.'

'I'm really sorry,' said Adam in a small voice.

'So am I,' said Eve in an even smaller voice.

'And so am I,' said God. 'And I forgive you. But there are some things that can't be undone. And although you will have to leave the garden, it doesn't mean that I won't go on loving and caring for you.'

So Adam and Eve sadly left the Garden of Eden. God sent an angel to guard the gate to make sure they did not return and, as a punishment for the snake, made him slide along the ground.

Adam blamed Eve and she blamed the snake. So did everyone else.

'You've got it all wrong,' the snake kept insisting. 'I didn't even touch the fruit. I tried telling that to the angel, but he just shook his wings and flashed his bright sword and said he'd had his orders from God. It's so unfair! Why did God punish me? It wasn't my fault!'

No one believed him.

And after all that, the snake thought bitterly, he had never even got to taste the fruit of that forbidden tree. It was just so unfair.

2

Mrs Noah's Cat

God was sad—the beautiful world he had created had become an evil place, full of wicked and selfish people. He decided to send rain to flood the world, so he could make a fresh start. The flood would destroy everything... except for one man, Noah, and his family, for Noah was a good man who loved God. And God also planned to save two of every living creature. So he told Noah to build a special boat big enough to keep them all safe when the flood waters rose.

Mrs Noah's cat was a large cat. She had brown fur, white paws and a bushy tail.

Mrs Noah's cat was in charge of Mrs Noah, Mr Noah, their sons, Shem, Ham and Japheth, their sons' wives, Mr Noah's dog, Mr Noah's vineyard and everything else that strayed on to Mr Noah's land.

Day after day she stalked round her territory,

terrifying the mice that lived in the walls and causing any birds who were building nests in Mr Noah's trees to take their twigs elsewhere. Mrs Noah's cat was good at climbing trees.

Nothing stirred on Mr Noah's land without her knowing about it. Her ever-twitching whiskers discovered what was happening as soon as it happened; she could smell out news before a word had been whispered; and her keen eyes could detect even the smallest ant scurrying along under Mr Noah's vines.

So it was extraordinary, to say the least, that Mrs Noah's cat was the very last to hear about God's message to Mr Noah—the message that was to change all their lives.

'What's this I hear about God wanting you to build a boat,' she demanded of Mr Noah, 'and why was I not told about it?' The fur on her back stood up in annoyance.

'Well you see, Tiddles,' said Mr Noah apologetically, 'I don't think you were nearby when God talked to me, and anyway it's an ark and not a boat.'

'Ark, boat, it's all the same,' retorted Mrs Noah's cat. 'It's something that floats on the water, isn't it? As we're miles from the sea, I really can't see what God's on about. And don't call me Tiddles,' she added.

Mrs Noah had chosen the name, much to her cat's dismay. It lacked dignity, it lacked presence—and

Mrs Noah's cat was sure she had plenty of both.

'God told me that he would have to destroy the world and every living creature, for it has become a wicked place,' Mr Noah explained. 'But he will save all our family and two of every animal, insect and bird.'

'How can we trust what God says?' asked Mrs Noah's cat, who did not trust anyone. Nobody, she felt—not even God—could be trusted to manage things as well as she did.

'I've trusted God all my life and he's never let me down,' Mr Noah replied simply. 'He told me to build an ark, so that we can live on it until the flood is over. Not,' Mr Noah went on, a worried look on his face, 'that I know anything at all about ark-building.'

Mrs Noah's cat stalked off, her tail in the air, and informed anyone who was in earshot that of course she had known about this ark long before God had spoken to Mr Noah, and that God had no need to tell *her* about wickedness. Wasn't she forever complaining about the bad behaviour of everyone in the nearby town?

The ark was built by Mr Noah's sons under the supervision of their father. In fact, it was under the supervision of Mrs Noah's cat. Mr Noah, as he had already admitted, knew nothing at all about ark-building. Mrs Noah's cat declared that she knew everything about it.

Animals, insects and birds arrived in pairs and Mrs Noah's cat stood at the head of the gangway, graciously allowing them in, after explaining that although Mr Noah appeared to be in charge under God, in reality she, Mrs Noah's cat, was in charge.

'I have,' she said loftily, 'a very special relationship with God.'

'But has God a special relationship with you?' asked one of the two foxes, unimpressed.

'God has a special relationship with all of us,' said a harassed Mr Noah.

'And especially with me,' said Mrs Noah's cat smugly.

The two foxes laughed and entered the ark, and two by two, the animals, insects and birds arrived and their names were ticked off by Mr Noah from a long list.

But when a single, thin, bedraggled ginger tom cat,

with one chewed ear and a mangy coat walked up the gangway, Mrs Noah's cat barred his way, hissing.

'This ark is for couples only,' she said firmly. 'Not for the likes of you.'

'Now, now,' said Mr Noah. 'The cat is a partner for you. God said there must be two of every creature on board.'

'For me?' Mrs Noah's cat was outraged. 'Couldn't you have found a more worthy partner? A Persian or a Siamese perhaps?'

'What's wrong with me?' asked the ginger tom. 'I know I look a bit knocked about on the outside, but it's the inside what matters—isn't it, Mr Noah?'

'I didn't make the choice, Tiddles,' said Mr Noah hastily. 'God did.'

'DON'T CALL ME TIDDLES!!' screeched Mrs Noah's cat. Turning to the ginger tom, she hissed and spat for all she was worth, but it was no use— Mr Noah had already ushered him on board. So with a disdainful sniff she disappeared into Mrs Noah's cabin, and there she stayed.

The rest of the animals arrived, the ark's great door was shut and, true to God's word, it started to rain.

After a few days of terrorizing Mrs Noah, her cat began to get bored.

'How long is this journey going to take?' she asked.

'Forty days and forty nights,' said Mrs Noah. 'That's what God told Mr Noah. At least, that's how

23

long it's going to rain. Then I suppose we've got to wait until the flood goes down and that could take for ever.'

Mrs Noah's cat sniffed.

'It's not my fault,' said Mrs Noah crossly. 'It's no good blaming me. No one asked me if I wanted to come. I married a farmer, not a sailor.' She looked dismally at her cat. 'Are you planning to spend the whole time in my cabin?'

Her cat stared at her.

'*Your* cabin?' she hissed.

'Our cabin,' said Mrs Noah hastily.

Mrs Noah's cat thought that if they were going to be at sea for a long time, she ought to explore the ark and reassert her authority. She was, after all, in charge. She was also getting rather tired of Mrs Noah's constant grumbles. So she left the cabin and began to stalk around the decks.

She saw large animals and small animals, ugly and good-looking ones. There were wild animals, tame animals, reptiles and insects, beasts and birds. She felt superior to them all.

But then she saw the lion.

Mrs Noah's cat stopped dead.

'And who might you be?' she said in a voice that was meant to sound bossy, but came out as a slightly strangled squeak.

The lion lifted his great head.

'I,' he said grandly, 'am in charge.'

Mrs Noah's cat drew herself up to her full height, arched her back and waved her tail in the air.

'No,' she said in a firmer voice. 'You've got that wrong. I am in charge.'

The lion looked down from his great height at Mrs Noah's cat and smiled. It was not a friendly smile.

'Listen, pussy,' he said. 'I could make a meal of you with one mouthful. I am King of the Jungle, Lord of all Beasts, and I AM IN CHARGE!'

Mrs Noah's cat took one step back and hissed.

The lion snarled and showed his set of very fine teeth.

What would have happened next is hard to imagine if a small ball of ginger fur had not hurled itself right under the lion's nose. It was the tom cat.

'Now look here, both of you,' he said, 'you need your heads knockin' together, you do! Neither of you's in charge. God's in charge, see, and he put Mr Noah in charge under him! Mr Noah said we've all got to get on while we're on the ark and that's what we're all goin' to do. I'll fight anyone who doesn't! Got it?'

The lion sighed. 'You're right of course,' he said in his grand voice, 'but it's not natural,' and he slunk away.

The ginger tom turned to Mrs Noah's cat.

'Now you come with me Tiddles, and stop making a fool of yourself!'

Mrs Noah's cat opened her mouth for an angry reply, but something stopped her from saying

anything. Although she would never have admitted it, she had been badly frightened by her meeting with the lion. She suddenly realized that, although she was in charge of everything on land, perhaps on the ark things were different. Especially when there were animals like the lion around.

'Perhaps,' she said, 'I'm not in charge on the ark.'

The ginger tom looked at her with affection.

'You're not in charge anywhere, Tiddles,' he said. 'God is.'

Mrs Noah's cat looked at the ginger tom. He did not look so bad now that he had been eating regular meals. And he had, after all, come to her rescue.

'Don't call me...' she began to say in a softer voice, then stopped again. Perhaps Tiddles wasn't such a

bad name after all. It was better than being known as Mrs Noah's cat.

It rained for forty days and forty nights. During that time, Mrs Noah's cat, now officially called Tiddles, and the ginger tom, who did not have a name, lived on the ark and became the greatest of friends.

When the rain had stopped and the flood waters had gone down, Tiddles and the ginger tom left the ark and stared at the bright, fresh world around them. The sun shone warmly on their backs and a gentle wind ruffled their fur. But all of a sudden, clouds swept across the sky and it began to rain.

'Is the flood starting again?' asked Tiddles.

'No,' said Mr Noah. 'Just look up!'

Tiddles and the ginger tom looked up and saw the

clouds part high above them. There, in a perfect arc that stretched across the sky, flamed the colours of a rainbow—red, orange, yellow, green, blue, indigo and violet. The cats gasped.

'God sent that rainbow as a sign that he will never send a flood to destroy the world again,' said Mr Noah. 'That's God's promise to us.'

For a long while Tiddles and the ginger tom sat together, staring at the rainbow. Then the rain stopped, the sun grew brighter, and the two cats began to set up a new home on dry land with Mr and Mrs Noah and their family.

3

The Swift Flies Too High

*Once upon a time, the people of the world had only one
language. After many years of wandering, they settled on a
plain in Babylon and decided to build a tower. It was to be
a tall tower, one that would reach the sky, one that would
reach heaven itself! But God had other ideas...*

The birds watched with interest as the men began to
dig the foundations.

'What are they doing?' asked the swift.

'Building,' said the eagle.

'Are they building a nest?'

They flew down to the building site to speak with
the men, for in those days men, animals and birds
shared a common language and could speak with
one another.

'What are you building?' the swift asked the man

in charge. 'Is it a big nest for a lot of chicks?'

'No,' said the man in charge. 'It's a tower.'

'A tall tower,' said a second man. 'The tallest in the world.'

'What's it for?' asked the eagle.

The men looked at one another.

'I don't think it's for anything,' said a third man, scratching his head. 'It's just going to be tall.'

'I don't understand,' said the swift. 'I build a nest to be a home and a place where my chicks can grow up. If the tower isn't a nest, what is it?'

'No one's going to live in it,' said the man in charge, 'We're building it to reach heaven.'

'Why?'

'Because we can,' said the second man.

'It's a challenge,' said the third man.

'How do you know heaven is up there?' asked the eagle. 'I've flown higher than the clouds and I've never seen any sign of it.'

'You're only a bird,' said the man in charge. 'You wouldn't know what heaven looked like if you flew right into it. We're cleverer than birds.'

'Maybe,' said the eagle, 'but you don't have wings and you can't fly.'

'If we can reach heaven, then we'll be as important as God,' the second man boasted.

'More important,' said the man in charge.

'We can't be more important, for God made us,'

said the eagle. 'We wouldn't be here at all if it wasn't for God.'

'That's what everyone says,' said the man in charge. 'But how do we know it's the truth? If we could get to heaven, we could find out.'

'I don't think people are cleverer than birds,' said the swift, after the men had returned to their work.

'Neither do I,' said the eagle, closing his eyes. 'I think they're very stupid.'

'But they do have a point,' said the swift. 'Wouldn't it be nice to find heaven?'

The eagle opened his eyes. 'It would be foolish even to try.'

'Why?'

'Because heaven is where God is, and if God wants us to see it, we will. If he doesn't, we won't. It's as simple as that.'

The swift did not quite believe this but he did not say anything, for the eagle had closed his eyes once more and gone to sleep.

The birds were not the only ones interested in the building. People and animals came from all parts of the plain to marvel at it.

'Can we offer our services?' asked a mole. 'We're very good at burrowing.'

The man in charge laughed. 'You? Listen, mole, we have thousands upon thousands of strong men building this tower. We don't need moles.'

'Just thought I'd ask.'

Once the foundations were laid, the tower began to rise. Ten, twenty, thirty storeys high, and still it kept rising. The birds flew in and out of its windows and settled on the top.

'It's a wonderful view, isn't it?' said the swift.

'No better than the one we get in mid-flight,' sniffed the eagle.

More and more people came to work on the tower and it quickly doubled and trebled in size. Soon its top had pierced the clouds, and a passing wagtail flew straight into it and was knocked unconscious.

'Never saw it till the last minute,' she said when she came round, 'and I didn't have time to turn. Gave me the surprise of my life, I can tell you. What is it, anyway?'

'It's a tower,' said the swift.

'It's a danger to us birds, if you ask me.'

'They're building it high enough to reach heaven,' the swift went on.

'I bet God'll have something to say about that,' said the wagtail, unimpressed.

'Do you think he'll send a thunderbolt to knock it down?' asked the swift.

'I haven't the faintest idea.'

'How are you feeling?' asked the eagle, flying down to join them.

'Rotten. I've a thumping great headache,' complained the wagtail.

'I think we birds should fly to heaven before those men get there,' said the swift.

'I don't know about that,' said the wagtail, gently flapping her bruised wings. 'But I think they should put some warning lights on that tower!'

When the tower reached forty storeys, the swift made a decision. He soared into the air.

'I don't care what you say!' he called down to the eagle. 'I'm going to fly to heaven!'

The tower, which had seemed so tall from the ground, soon grew smaller as the swift climbed higher and higher.

He laughed out loud. 'How stupid men are! I've already reached twice its height!'

Night fell, and the swift flew higher still. He turned his head from side to side, but could see

33

nothing other than the velvety black of the sky, studded with brilliant white stars.

The swift was very tired when daylight came. The sun rose and its rays burned hot on his wings. He looked up, but could only see the deep blue sky arching above him. There was no sign of heaven.

At last he could fly no further. Worn out with tiredness, hunger and thirst, the swift let himself be carried downwards on the wind, and fell to earth with a thump, right at the eagle's feet.

'Well?' asked the eagle.

'You were right,' said the swift. 'Heaven's not up there. And I've burned my wings flying too close to the sun.'

When the tower reached fifty storeys high, the workmen held a feast to which they invited all the animals, insects and birds.

'What do you think now?' asked the man in charge proudly.

'I think that God won't like it,' said the eagle.

That night the entire tower was wreathed in dark cloud. The following morning, the man in charge woke up and jumped to his feet.

'Come on you lazy lot!' he called. 'Up with you!'

As the men began to wake, a babble of noise arose. Overnight, it seemed, a hundred different languages had sprung up.

'We've another two storeys to build today!' the man in charge called, but no one understood him. The workmen looked at one another, frightened and confused.

'What's he saying?'

'I don't understand!'

'What's happened?'

No one could understand anyone else's language!

'We've got to start work!' shouted the man in charge, but instead of working, arguments and fights broke out all over the site. The workmen began running away, and the man in charge sat down on a stone and burst into tears.

'I said God wouldn't like it,' murmured the eagle.

'It's better than a thunderbolt,' said the swift.

The ground heaved and a very dusty mole appeared.

'I've been trying to find you,' he said to the man in charge. 'I thought you'd like to know that I and my colleagues have been carrying out a survey of the foundations.'

'What's that?'

'They're not secure,' the mole continued.

'I don't understand.'

The mole sighed. 'The tower could fall down any moment.'

But it seemed that men could no longer understand the language of the birds, the animals or the insects either.

Within an hour there was no one left at the tower. Even the man in charge had run away.

The eagle looked up and a shaft of sunlight pierced through the clouds and shone on the very top of the tower.

'I think God wanted to teach men a lesson,' he said, 'to show that he's in charge and not them.'

There was a loud rumble. The earth shook and the tower fell down. The eagle turned to the swift.

'Do you think they'll learn their lesson?' he asked.

4

The Speckled Goat

Jacob was a trickster. He had deceived his father and his brother. He fled from his home to his Uncle Laban, but Laban was also a trickster. After fourteen years of hard work with no wages, Jacob believed God wanted him to return home. But he had no flock or wealth of his own to take with him, and Laban had other ideas...

The crow flew low over the field.

'Laban has offered to pay wages to his nephew!' he shouted to the flock of sheep and goats.

'So what?' mumbled one of the sheep, busy nibbling away at a patch of grass.

'I thought you'd be interested,' said the crow huffily.

'I am,' said the young speckled goat, who was interested in everything. 'Why is our master offering to pay wages now, if he's never paid them before?'

'I don't know,' said the crow. 'I'll find out.'

He returned with more news.

'Jacob wants to go home, so his uncle's offered him wages to persuade him to stay,' he said.

The nanny goat looked up. 'I hope he doesn't go,' she said. 'I like Jacob. He looks after us so well. I don't want him to leave.'

'I don't see what all the fuss is about,' said the oldest goat. 'Laban's trying to bribe his nephew, that's all. It's no more than I'd have expected from such a man, and it doesn't affect any of us.'

'Jacob has asked Laban if he can have all the speckled, striped and spotted goats as wages,' the crow continued. 'And the black lambs as well.'

Laban's flock of sheep and goats looked at one another in astonishment.

'But there's only a handful of us speckled, striped and spotted goats,' said the speckled goat.

'And two black lambs,' said one of them.

'Not enough to make a decent flock,' the speckled goat continued. 'I don't think that's proper wages at all.'

'Jacob's a fool,' said a sheep.

'I don't think he's a fool at all,' said the oldest goat slowly. 'I think he's being very cunning. I expect he has a plan.'

'I'll find out what it is,' said the crow, and flew away.

'Why should Jacob have a plan?' asked the speckled goat.

'Because he's a tricky customer,' said the oldest goat. 'Deceitful.'

The speckled goat was confused. 'I thought his uncle was deceitful.'

'They both are,' said the oldest goat. 'It probably runs in the family. Years ago, Jacob cheated his brother, Esau. That's why he had to run away from home and ended up working for his uncle.'

'He was much younger then,' protested the nanny goat, 'and I'm sure he's learnt his lesson.'

'Once a baddy, always a baddy, I say,' said the oldest goat stubbornly.

'I heard that God spoke to Jacob in a dream and promised to look after him,' said the nanny goat. 'So God must be fond of Jacob.'

'Why?' asked the speckled goat.

'God probably sees something in him that the oldest goat can't,' said the nanny goat.

The crow came swooping back.

'Jacob told his sons to take the speckled, spotted and striped goats over to the good grazing land away from the farm.'

'What about the black lambs?' asked the black lamb anxiously.

The crow was not listening. 'He said that God has promised to help them build up a large, strong flock, so that they can all go home.'

'I don't mind where I go, as long as the grazing's

good,' said the nanny goat.

The young speckled goat did not agree. He wandered away from the flock and began to climb the hillside.

'I don't want to leave my home,' he thought. 'And I'm not sure I want to go with Jacob either, even if he's not as bad as the oldest goat says.'

He looked up at the crow, who was flying above him.

'You're clever, crow,' he said politely. 'What can I do to stay on the farm with Laban?'

'You can try losing your speckles.'

The speckled goat looked around. The hillside was dotted with low, spiky bushes. Perhaps, he thought, he could rub his speckles away. He plunged into the thorny tangle of bushes and began to rub his back against the sharp spikes.

'Whatever are you doing?' asked the crow.

'I'm trying to lose my speckles,' said the speckled goat. 'Ouch! It hurts!'

The crow began to laugh. He laughed so much that he fell off his rock. 'You can't lose your speckles by rubbing them off,' he said.

'Can't you? Oh.'

The speckled goat tore himself free of the bushes and plunged deep into a nearby pool of water to ease his scratched and sore back. He looked at his reflection in the water and had another idea. Perhaps he could wash his speckles away.

The crow flew down and perched on the branch of a tree.

'What are you doing?' he asked.

'Washing my speckles away,' the speckled goat replied.

The crow laughed so much that he fell off his branch and landed, with a splash, in the pool.

'It's no laughing matter,' said the speckled goat. 'I don't want to leave my home and go with Jacob, even if the grazing is good.'

'Why not?' asked the crow. 'You'll be all right with him. God's on his side. But if you really don't want to go, why don't you just trick Jacob and his uncle into thinking you're not speckled any more.'

How do I do that?'

'I can't think of everything,' said the crow, and flew away.

The speckled goat walked into the hills thinking about what the crow had said. The sun shone down on the bare rocks and white chalky soil. The speckled goat stopped, looked at the dusty road, then rolled over and over. Soon all his speckles were covered by a film of white chalky dust.

He returned to the farm to find the sheep and goats being divided.

'Plain for you, plain for you, plain for you, spotted for me,' said Jacob as he separated the goats.

'White for you, white for you, white for you, white for you and black for me,' he went on, separating the two black lambs from the rest of the flock.

Laban watched, a pleased smile on his face. He was getting the better bargain as there were far more white sheep than black, and most of the goats were plain.

'Plain for you...' said Jacob, sending the disguised speckled goat over to Laban's side of the field.

But at that moment, the sky darkened and it began to pour with rain. As everyone watched, the speckled goat's coat of white dust was gently washed away.

The sheep and the goats began to laugh, as did the

crow, who was flying overhead. Jacob walked over to the speckled goat and gently herded him across to his side of the field.

'You're part of my flock now, and I'll look after you,' he said quietly. 'I'm sorry to be moving you to a new pasture, but God's promised me that it'll be a better one where I can build a large flock of sheep and goats of my own. And then I'll be going home, even though my uncle doesn't want me to go. But it's what God wants that matters.' He laughed. 'Uncle Laban thinks I'm stupid to have taken so few of the flock for my wages, but it's all part of God's plan and I trust in what God tells me.'

Later that evening the speckled goat munched contentedly on fresh grass. Perhaps the nanny goat had been right, he thought. Perhaps Jacob couldn't be that bad, not if God was on his side.

'And I'd rather be on the side that God's on, than any other,' he said out loud.

5

The Frog and the Pharaoh

God's people, the Israelites, were slaves in Egypt and God wanted them to be set free. But Pharaoh, the ruler of Egypt, refused to let them go. So God sent a number of plagues on the whole land. After each one, Pharaoh promised God's prophet, Moses, that he would set the Israelites free. But each time, Pharaoh changed his mind. One of the plagues was frogs...

It all happened very quickly. One moment the green tree frog was sitting on a branch of his favourite tree, minding his own business and enjoying the peace, the silence and the cool evening air, and the next moment...

... WHOOSH!

The frog found himself squatting on a dusty bank beside a river. It was a strange river, for instead of water, a sticky red liquid flowed sluggishly between its banks. A hot sun beat uncomfortably on his skin. There was no green grass and no trees... but there were frogs.

Lining both sides of the river were thousands upon thousands of frogs of all colours, shapes and sizes. Green frogs like himself, brown frogs, golden, crimson, mottled, speckled, spotted and striped. There were small frogs, large ones, bullfrogs, cricket frogs, narrow and wide-mouthed frogs. There was even a troupe of flying frogs!

The green tree frog had never seen so many frogs before.

What could have happened, he wondered? Was it indigestion, caused by eating a large and tasty meal of assorted flies? Was it some sort of surprise holiday thought up by his great-nephew, who was always saying he was a stick-in-the-mud and ought to have adventures? But the tree frog was just a middle-aged, middle-sized frog who liked the peace and quiet of his own home.

'Where am I?' he asked out loud.

A broad-horned frog turned his beady eyes on him. 'Egypt. Beside the River Nile.'

'Seems a funny sort of river to me,' the tree frog said. 'What's all that red stuff?'

'Blood,' croaked an enormous bull frog in a deep voice.

'Oh.'

'Never used to be like that,' the bull frog went on. 'Used to be a beautiful river. I've bathed in it many times.'

'It was that man Moses,' said a Golden Arrow poison frog coming up behind. 'Him and his brother, Aaron.'

'What did they do?' the tree frog asked nervously. He had never spoken with a poison frog before.

'They struck the water with a stick and it turned to blood.'

'Why did they do that?'

'To teach the Egyptians a lesson,' the poison frog said, licking his lips.

The tree frog fell silent. It was not a good idea, he thought, to ask too many questions of a poison frog.

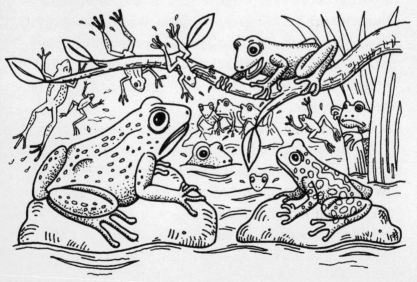

The bull frog hopped onto a stone and raised his voice.

'Now then, frogs,' he croaked, 'we've been called here to do a job!'

The frogs cheered.

'We've got to put the fear of God into Pharaoh so he'll let the Israelites go free!'

The frogs cheered louder.

'Anyone got any ideas?'

'Let's hop into the Egyptians' houses!' shouted a cricket frog in a shrill voice.

'Hide in their beds!' croaked a reed frog.

'Fly in their faces!' called a flying frog.

The frogs were jumping up and down with excitement.

'We'll invade the palace…!' squeaked a bush squeaker frog.

'… and frighten Pharaoh!' called a tiny frog in a small voice.

The poison frog laughed. 'You wouldn't scare anyone,' he said scornfully.

'All right then, frogs,' roared the bull frog. 'Jump to it!'

With more cheers the frogs began to move towards a town a short distance away.

'Excuse me,' said the tree frog, 'but I think there's been some mistake.'

'No mistake,' said the bull frog. 'We've had our

orders from Moses and he's had his orders from God. God's trying to free his people from slavery.'

'They're treated very badly,' said the poison frog. 'Beaten and starved.'

'Pharaoh won't let them leave Egypt because they do all the work,' the bull frog went on. 'He won't even let them worship God. So God says to Moses, "See here, Moses, you've got to do something about this, because the Israelites are my people and I care for them. I'll be right behind you, and I'll throw in a few fancy touches as well, like turning the water into blood and bringing a plague of frogs." That's what God said.'

'How do you know what God said?' asked the poison frog.

'I heard Moses telling his brother,' said the bull frog.

The tree frog was getting impatient. 'I'm sure it's a worthy cause,' he said, 'but it's nothing to do with me. I've no quarrel with this Pharaoh, whoever he is, or his Egyptians, whoever they are. So, if you'd be kind enough to tell me how to get home, I wish you the best of luck and I'm sure you'll succeed in whatever it is you're trying to do.'

'I think,' said the poison frog, 'that it's time we went to the town.'

The tree frog went along with them. You don't argue with a poison frog.

The town was in uproar. Frogs were everywhere,

surging through the streets, jumping in, on, over and under everything. Terrified Egyptians were racing out of their homes and streaming from the palace, falling over each other in their hurry to get away.

'Never had so much fun in all my life,' said a large striped frog, wiping her bulging eyes. 'Boo!' she yelled at a fleeing palace guard.

'Gotcha!' croaked a flying frog jumping onto his head. The guard burst into tears and fell to the ground.

The tree frog took one look, then turned and began to hop away. He was going to find his way home, with or without help.

A shadow fell across his path. Two men were approaching and one was carrying a stout stick. They did not seem at all scared of the mass of frogs still jumping up and down the street.

They must be Moses and his brother, the tree frog thought, the ones who started it all.

The men squatted in the dusty road and the tree frog squatted beside them. He had an idea. If Moses and Aaron were the people who had summoned the frogs, then maybe they would help him get back home. If he asked very nicely, of course. He listened to what they were saying.

'Do you think it will work?' Aaron asked. 'Will Pharaoh let our people go?'

'If that's what God wants,' said Moses. 'God doesn't make mistakes. Although I thought he had when he chose me to lead his people out of Egypt. Why me, I asked? I'll be no good. I get all mixed up and start to stammer when I get nervous. But God has his reasons, and you speak for me when I get tongue-tied.'

The brothers were silent for a moment, then Moses got to his feet. 'Come on. Let's get it over with. Let's go and see if Pharaoh has had enough of the frogs.'

The tree frog gave a hop, and found himself clinging to the top of Aaron's stout stick.

He opened his mouth to speak, then shut it again. Later, he thought. He would ask later. For he suddenly thought that it would be a shame to go home, having come all this way, without seeing Pharaoh, the ruler of Egypt. What a story he'd have to tell his great-nephew! So the tree frog clung tightly to Aaron's stick and went to the palace.

They found Pharaoh sitting on his throne, surrounded by frogs, who croaked menacingly whenever he moved.

'Well, Ph-Pharaoh?' Moses asked, beginning to stammer.

'You can't frighten me with frogs,' said Pharaoh scornfully. 'Why, any magician can summon them up. Surely you can do better than that!'

But he is frightened, thought the tree frog. Despite his brave talk, I think he's frightened. Perhaps he is afraid of frogs.

The tree frog suddenly felt very brave and pleased that he had decided to stay.

'I'm n-not trying to f-frighten you,' said Moses. 'I'm carrying out G-God's orders. He has a m-message for you. He said, "Let my people g-go".'

Pharaoh laughed.

Moses took Aaron's stout stick, with the tree frog still clinging to the top, and held it up.

Now the tree frog had never fallen off a branch in his life. He had suckers to help him cling on. But as

Moses raised the stick, the tree frog suddenly lost his grip. He panicked, jumped… and landed right in Pharaoh's lap.

Pharaoh let out a great scream.

'All right! You win! I'll let the Israelites go!'

'When?' asked Moses.

'Tomorrow,' said Pharaoh, shuddering. 'Only tell your God to take the frogs away!'

Moses and Aaron left the Palace with smiles on their faces. The tree frog was with them, and he was smiling, too. The following day Moses asked God to take all the frogs away…

… and the tree frog found himself back on a branch of his favourite tree, and things were just as they were. Or not quite.

For although the green tree frog could have done without the adventure, he was quite proud of himself for playing a part in changing the mind of the king of Egypt. Not that his great-nephew believed him. He said his great-uncle must have been dreaming.

6

The Complaining Cow

Pharaoh finally allowed the Israelites to leave Egypt, and Moses led them into the desert. It was the start of a journey to God's Promised Land. Moses believed that God would look after his people, provide them with food and water and show them the way they should go. The Israelites were tired and frightened, and many of them grumbled and doubted. But God kept his word, sometimes in surprising ways...

'Isn't it exciting?' the cream cow said to her sister, as they set off from their home. 'I never thought Pharaoh would let us go.' She did not wait for an answer. 'It was all so sudden.'

The two cows joined the crowd of people, sheep, goats and other animals as they headed for the desert.

'I do think Moses is amazing,' said the cream cow, skipping along happily. 'Just look at him, striding out there in front of us. He brought down those plagues on the Egyptians. He's quite my hero.'

'I thought God did it,' said her sister, but the cream cow was not listening.

'I did laugh when those frogs came,' she said. 'Quite polite they were, really, although how they frightened the Egyptians! I didn't like the plague of flies though. I think flies are very rude.'

The cream cow walked on in silence for a moment. 'Where do you think we're going?' she asked.

'A new country,' her sister said. 'A land promised by God.'

'What fun!'

The Israelites left the fertile lands of Egypt and entered the desert. The soil was thin and poor. There was little grass and only a few bushes.

Two vultures began circling overhead.

'What do you think?' asked one of them.

'I'm thinking there's a lot of tasty dinners walking along down there,' said the other.

'That's what I'm thinking.'

The cream cow stumbled on a rock. She was growing tired.

'Is it much further?' she complained. 'I'm tired and I'm thirsty and there's no decent grass to eat.'

'There will be,' said her sister, 'in the Promised Land.'

'Promises are all very well,' muttered the cream cow. 'But you can't eat or drink promises.'

Text copyright © 2001 Avril Rowlands
Illustrations copyright © 2001 Rosslyn Moran
This edition copyright © 2001 Lion Publishing

The moral rights of the author and illustrator
have been asserted

Published by
Lion Publishing plc
Sandy Lane West, Oxford, England
www.lion-publishing.co.uk
ISBN 0 7459 4458 2

First edition 2001
10 9 8 7 6 5 4 3 2 1

A catalogue record for this book is available
from the British Library

Typeset in 12/16 ZapfCalligraphic
Printed and bound in Great Britain by
Omnia Books Ltd, Glasgow

The crowd was walking more slowly now, the people weighed down by their household possessions, the animals struggling for footholds among the rocks. They came to a halt on the top of a hill. The desert stretched before them, a scrubby land of rock and sand, shimmering under the hot midday sun. Moses looked up at the sky.

'Which way, O Lord?' he asked.

The cream cow nudged her sister. 'Doesn't he know the way?'

'He's asking God for help,' her sister replied. 'We're in God's hands.'

'He ought to know the way,' the cream cow complained. 'I mean, I wouldn't have come on this expedition if I'd known that Moses didn't have a clue where we're going. Promised Land indeed! That's humans for you. All talk. Do you know, sister, I think we should go home. It wasn't that bad in Egypt after all. Our masters and mistresses might have been slaves, but that didn't really affect us, did it? I'm sure we'd find a new master and mistress, and better grass, too.'

She stopped, for a great column of cloud had suddenly risen in front of her.

'Storm coming up,' she said. 'That's all we need.'

'I don't think it's a storm,' her sister replied. 'I think it's God giving Moses directions.'

Moses began walking towards the cloud and the

Israelites followed. All day they walked and the cloud moved ahead of them.

The two vultures began to get impatient.

'Come on, drop down dead,' one of them urged. 'Human, sheep, cow, I'm not fussy. I'll even eat goat at a pinch. My mum brought me up to eat anything.'

It began to grow dark.

'Why doesn't Moses let us rest?' moaned the cream cow. 'There's no point walking in the dark. We can't see where we're going.'

'Look,' said her sister.

In front of them rose a tall column of fire.

'So someone's having a bonfire,' the cream cow said sarcastically. 'How interesting!'

'I think it's God showing us the way when it's dark and we can't see the cloud.'

'Know-all,' muttered the cream cow.

Day after day the Israelites and their animals walked through the desert, following the column of cloud by day and the column of fire by night.

Day after day the two vultures flew overhead.

Day after day the cream cow carried on complaining. 'When are we going to see this Promised Land, that's what I want to know? Does it really exist, I ask myself? We've been told it's a land flowing with milk and honey. Well, speaking as a cow, it certainly won't flow with milk unless there's good grazing when we get there, and as for honey...

I never liked the stuff myself. Very overrated. I can't think what the bees see in it.'

Her sister plodded on, saying nothing.

'I blame Moses,' said the cream cow. 'His brother's no better. Two of a kind. You know, sister, I always thought there was something a bit funny about them. Didn't I say many times that there was something funny about those two? I don't like to say "I told you so", but I always thought there was something funny…'

The vultures flew lower.

'You know what?' said one of them.

'No.'

'They're growing thinner by the day.'

'Pity. I could do with some meat.'

Later that day the Israelites came to a vast stretch of water—the Sea of Reeds. Everyone stopped, while Moses walked to the water's edge.

'And how are we meant to cross that sea?' asked the cream cow sarcastically. 'Are we supposed to fly? Is God going to give us all wings, do you suppose?'

'Perhaps he'll provide some boats,' said her sister.

'If you think I'm stepping into some rickety, ramshackle old boat that's likely to sink, you've another think coming,' snapped the cream cow.

The two vultures, black shapes against the sun, circled the waiting crowds lazily.

'Soon, don't you think?' asked one.

'About time too, if you ask me,' said the other. 'I'm starving.'

The crowds and the animals were silent—apart from the cream cow.

'What's Moses doing?'

'Talking to God I expect,' said her sister.

'Well, I've had enough of this talking,' said the cream cow. 'Talking doesn't give me good grazing. I'm off home.'

With that she turned and began running back across the desert.

The vultures wheeled.

'That's the one!'

'Had my eye on her for some time, I have,' said the other, looking at her hungrily.

The cream cow had not travelled very far before she heard horses. She stopped. She heard distant shouts and cries. Then she saw them, a small black cloud on the horizon. The Egyptian army.

The vultures swooped lower.

'Egyptians,' one of them remarked. 'How nice. That means there'll be a battle. I do like a battle.'

'Lots of lovely pickings,' said the other.

The cream cow turned and ran back the way she had come. Her hooves slipped and slithered over the rough stones and her breath came in great sobbing gasps. She stopped, looked up and stared in amazement.

Moses had lifted his great stick high over the Sea
of Reeds. A strong wind began to blow and, as the
cream cow watched, the waters were whipped into
two gigantic walls, leaving a clear pathway down the
middle. The Israelites, the cows, the sheep and the
goats began to cross, passing on dry land between
towering walls of water.

The cream cow found new strength.

'Wait!' she called. 'Wait for me! Don't go without me!'

She thundered towards them.

'Please wait! I take it all back! I'm sorry I ran away. I'm sorry I've been complaining. I won't do it again, but please, please don't leave me behind!'

She was the very last to cross. Trembling, she scrambled up the far bank.

'I'm so glad you made it,' said her sister placidly. 'I was quite worried.'

Moses raised his great stick and, with a crash, the wall of waves collapsed and the sea grew calm again.

The vultures wheeled away in disgust.

The Israelites began their walk once more.

'We're safe now, sister,' said the cream cow. 'I always said that Moses was a clever man. Him and God together, why, they're an unbeatable team! He trusts God and God always makes everything come out right. Promised Land, here we come!'

The cream cow's sister smiled to herself, but said nothing at all.

7

The Donkey and the Angel

King Balak, king of Moab, was worried when he heard that after many years' wandering in the desert, God's people, the Israelites, were close to his land. He was afraid that they would take over his kingdom. He wanted a curse put on them and summoned Balaam, a wise man, to his court. But Balaam was a man who trusted in God...

The old donkey was grazing peacefully in the meadow when her two grandsons raced up to her.

'Grandma,' said her eldest grandson, 'is it true?'

The old donkey looked up. 'Is what true?'

'About you and the angel,' said her eldest grandson.

'And how your master was a fool who used to beat you black and blue,' added her youngest.

The old donkey snorted. 'Has that goat been

telling you stories?' she asked. 'You don't want to believe anything he says.'

'Didn't your master beat you?' asked her youngest grandson, disappointed.

'Only the once,' said the old donkey, 'and he was very sorry about it afterwards.'

'And wasn't he a fool?' asked her eldest grandson.

'We can all be fools at times,' said the old donkey slowly. 'And it wasn't altogether my master's fault, for he couldn't see the angel to begin with.'

'But he must have been a fool, otherwise he would have!'

'You'd argue the hind leg off a donkey, you would,' the old donkey said fondly. 'Don't be so quick to judge. If there's one thing I've learned in my life, it's that things aren't always as simple as they seem.'

'So what really happened, then?' asked her youngest grandson.

The old donkey munched thoughtfully on some grass before replying.

'It was like this,' she said at last. 'Balaam, my master, was a wise man and still is—God be praised—although old and frail now, like me. Perhaps he's wiser now than he was when we set out on that journey. His wisdom was so widely known that even the king would sometimes ask him for advice. When that happened, my master would saddle me up and climb on my back, and I would carry him to wherever the king happened to be at the time. As we journeyed, my master would sometimes sing, or talk to God. I liked those journeys very much.'

The old donkey fell silent.

'Weren't you afraid?' asked her youngest grandson. 'Going off round the country?'

'No, I was never afraid, for my master was a wise man. Besides, I had a fine set of sharp teeth in those days and a good kick in my legs, so I could take care of myself, and my master too if need be.'

Her grandsons looked her in disbelief, for they found it hard to believe that their grandmother could ever have been young and strong. Her teeth were now worn and blunted, and she moved slowly and painfully.

'But this time I didn't think we were going anywhere. King Balak had sent messengers, very grand ones, to ask my master to visit him and put a curse on the Israelites. The messengers told us that the Israelites had come from Egypt and were now close to the king's land. King Balak was afraid they meant to take the land for themselves and thought that one of my master's curses would stop them.

'The messengers came with a big bag of gold. I was there when they took it out of their saddlebags. I could see my master eyeing it and knew he was thinking that the money would come in very handy for a new roof. My master was never a rich man despite being so wise.'

'Why wasn't he rich?' demanded her eldest grandson. 'If I was a wise man, I'd get lots and lots of gold for myself.'

'Do you want to hear this story, or don't you?'

Her grandsons were silent.

'My master told the messengers that he would think about it and talk it over with God and have a reply by the morning. That night he had a dream, sent by God. He was told not to curse the people of Israel, for they were God's own people and under God's care.

'So that was that. No trip this time. Pity, I thought, for I liked to travel, but there would be other times. The messengers went away. But a few weeks later they were back. Not the same ones. No—the king had sent even grander ones than before. This time they brought with them two sackfuls of gold.' The old donkey stopped for a moment. 'And this time my master said yes.'

'Not such a fool, after all,' her eldest grandson remarked.

'Why did he say yes?' demanded her youngest grandson.

The old donkey was silent for a moment.

'My master had another dream, sent by God,' she said at last. 'He was told to get ready to go to the king, but not to set out or speak to the king before God told him to. But my master didn't wait for a further message from God. Instead he saddled up and rode off to the king straight away.'

'Was it because of the money?' asked her eldest grandson.

'Yes,' the old donkey said, then shook her head. 'No. I don't know. Perhaps my master was just curious to find out more. Perhaps he was swayed by the thought of the money—I must say, I could have done with a new roof to my stable. Perhaps he thought he knew better than God. At any rate, he disobeyed God's orders.'

'I think he was just greedy,' said her eldest grandson.

'We set out on our journey. My master was deep in thought and I guessed he was troubled in his mind. I trod as carefully as I could in order not to disturb him. Wise men need peace and quiet when they're troubled.'

'Why?'

'In order to think wise thoughts of course,' said the donkey shortly. 'It's just as well you two don't belong to a wise man, for you talk all the time!

'Well, there I was, watching the road ahead for potholes, and there was my master, lost in his thoughts, and that was why he didn't see what I saw. I stopped at once.

' "Look!" I said. but my master, wise as he was, didn't understand the language of donkeys. I was trembling and shaking and sweating all over, for there, right in the middle of the road...'

'... WAS AN ANGEL!' her grandsons shouted together.

The old donkey nodded. 'The angel was carrying a drawn sword in his hand and there was light all around him. I was terrified, and turned off the road into a field. I was too scared to try and pass him. My master was furious! That's when he did what he'd never done before. He hit me.

' "Can't you see?" I cried. "That's God's angel! I can't go riding straight through God's angel!" But of course my master couldn't understand and spurred me back to the road. The angel had vanished, but no sooner had the road narrowed to a path running between the high walls of some vineyards, than there he was again.'

'What did you do?'

'I pressed myself close to the wall to try and pass without getting in the angel's way. But my master's foot got crushed against the wall and he beat me again.'

'I wish I'd been there,' said her eldest grandson. 'I'd have thrown Balaam off my back and kicked him!'

'I didn't want to do that. I felt sorry for him.'

'Sorry for him?'

'You wouldn't understand,' the old donkey said gently. 'He's a good man really. A kind man. And although I was so frightened, I felt very proud to have seen an angel. It was a wonderful sight. It's not every donkey that sees an angel. I was just sorry my master couldn't see him as well.'

'What happened next?' asked her youngest grandson after a pause.

'The angel moved ahead and stood at the narrowest part of the road, so narrow there was no room to turn or squeeze past. So I did the only thing left. I lay down.

'My master was furious. "You worthless donkey!" he yelled. "I'll sell you as soon as I get to town! Now get up!" And he beat me again.

' "Why are you beating me for the third time?" I asked. "What have I done?"

'And, do you know, an amazing thing happened. My master understood what I was saying!

' "You've made a fool of me!" he shouted. "If I had a sword, I'd kill you!"

'Poor man, he was so angry.

' "Aren't I your own donkey, who you've always ridden?" I said. "Haven't I always carried you faithfully? Have I ever disobeyed you before?"

'Balaam, my master, burst into tears, threw the stick away and flung his arms around my neck. For at that moment...'

'... he saw the angel for himself!' said her eldest grandson triumphantly.

'And the angel told Balaam that you'd saved his life!' her youngest grandson added.

'If you know the story so well, why ask me?' said the old donkey, smiling, and she bent her head and began to munch placidly at the fresh green grass.

8

The Lamb and the Shepherd

King David was the greatest king Israel had ever known. Yet when he was a boy, he was just a shepherd, the youngest of his family, and spent his days looking after his father's flocks. He enjoyed singing and playing the harp, and made up many songs we now call 'psalms' in the Bible. David loved God and tried to follow God's wishes in all that he did. God had great plans for him and sent his prophet Samuel to find him...

The young lamb woke up, sniffed the fresh cool air and bounded into the field.

'Wake up, mother!' he bleated as he ran and jumped from one side to the other. 'It's a beautiful day!'

His mother watched him fondly and laughed. It was a beautiful day. The chill grip of winter was beginning to leave the land of Judah. There was still snow on the tops of the hills, but in the valleys, spring was beginning to stir. Fresh young leaves were opening on the trees, the grass was soft and juicy to eat and the sun's rays were warm on the sheep's back. It was a good-to-be-alive day!

'Don't stray too far, now!' she called. 'No further than the next field! You know what I told you!'

'I won't forget!' called the lamb.

But the minute he had run into the next field, he had forgotten his mother's advice about the dangers lurking in the hills. The sun glinted through the trees, speckling the grass with shifting patterns of gold on green.

My mother's an old fusspot, thought the lamb. There could be no danger on a day like today. Today would be a special day.

It was to be a special day for David, the young shepherd, although when he woke that morning he did not know just how special. David slept in the fields, close by his sheep. He had woken that morning with a new song running through his mind and, as he sat among his flock, he plucked the strings of his harp and began to sing:

'The Lord is my shepherd;
I have everything I need.
He lets me rest in fields of green grass
and leads me to quiet pools of fresh water.'

It was a hauntingly beautiful song and the lamb stopped for a moment to listen. But only for a moment. There was a whole new world to explore.

He found a stream, whose water bubbled over clean, shining pebbles. The sounds it made mingled with the song David was singing. The sun glinted on its surface. The lamb slipped on the grassy bank and bleated in surprise as the water splashed his woolly legs. Then he shook his head and bleated in excitement. The lamb was enjoying himself.

David was also enjoying himself, sitting among his flock, singing his new song. But he put down his harp and stood up when he saw the servant running towards him.

'Your father wants you home at once!'

'What about my flock? I can't just leave them.'

'I was told to look after them for you.'

'All right,' said David. 'But mind you keep a sharp watch and go after any sheep that stray from the fields.'

The lamb had grown tired of jumping in and out of the stream. For a moment he watched how the water wound down from the hills, like a silver thread, twisting and turning around rocks until it reached the level ground. Then he bleated in pleasure and began to follow it up the hillside.

David arrived home to find his father, Jesse, his mother and his seven brothers, all dressed in their finest clothes and ready to sit down to a feast.

'Ah, David,' said his father, 'we have a guest. The prophet Samuel has honoured us with his presence. He has asked to see you.'

'To see me?'

Samuel was an old man, with deep, dark eyes. He crossed the room and stood in front of David, staring at the boy. For a long moment no one spoke.

Then Samuel said, 'This is the boy.'

David's family all began to talk at once, but fell silent when Samuel raised his hand.

'God sent me to find a new king and this is the one,' he said

'But we already have a king,' said Jesse, 'King Saul.'

'David will be king after him,' said Samuel.

'But he's only a boy,' Jesse protested. 'My youngest. And he's a shepherd, not a king.'

'A king is shepherd of his people,' said Samuel.

Then David knelt down and Samuel anointed him with oil, as a sign that he would be king.

Back in the field, the lamb's mother was beginning to get worried. Where was her lamb? She searched from one end to the other, then went into the far field and began to search there, too.

'Come on out, if you're hiding!' she called. 'It's getting late.'

She began to run this way and that, but the lamb was nowhere to be found.

David, she thought. I must tell David. He'll know

what to do. He'll find my lamb, I know he will.

'My lamb has gone missing!' she cried, running up to the boy who was sitting against a rock.

It was not David.

The servant opened one eye and pushed the sheep away with his foot. 'Oh, go and bleat somewhere else,' he said crossly. 'I was just having a nice sleep.'

The lamb climbed higher and higher, following the stream right to its source. The sun was burning through his woolly coat and he was hot and thirsty. He bent his head to drink, slipped sideways and fell into a tangle of thorny brambles. He twisted this way and that, bleating loudly as he struggled to tear himself free. But the more he tried, the more entangled he became.

'Help me! Someone please help!'

'Well, hello,' said a voice.

The lamb struggled to turn around. Behind him stood a large and hungry wolf who grinned, revealing a set of razor-sharp teeth.

'That's quite a mess you've got yourself into.'

He took a step closer.

'We'd better get you free, hadn't we.'

'Oh, would you?' said the lamb gratefully.

'But of course. I can't eat you when you're all tangled up in that thicket.'

'Eat me?' said the lamb in a small voice.

The wolf began to tear at the vicious branches with his strong, white teeth.

'What a treat!' he said. 'I just knew this was going to be a specially good day when I woke up this morning!'

'P-p-please don't eat me.'

'Why not? You're food, aren't you?'

'I'm only small and won't make much of a meal.'

'True. But you're better than nothing.'

'Oh, please,' said the lamb. 'It's a lovely day. Don't spoil it.'

'But I won't be spoiling it,' said the wolf, smiling happily. 'On the contrary. I'll be making it even better. For me, that is.'

The feasting had just begun in Jesse's house when the sheep ran into the room, bleating wildly. Food was knocked off the table as she brushed past it, making straight for David. She butted him with her hard head.

David stood up. 'I have to go, Father.' He turned to Samuel. 'If God wants me to be king and shepherd of his people, then I will be. But right now I'm shepherd to my flock, and I think they need me.'

The wolf had nearly cleared away the brambles. The lamb watched his strong mouth and sharp teeth, and wondered whether being eaten would hurt much.

'I wish I'd listened to my mother,' the lamb sniffled. 'She warned me not to go on the hills.'

'Being eaten will teach you a lesson,' said the wolf.

He laughed. 'But I'm afraid it'll be too late for you to learn from it.'

He tore aside the last of the branches and opened his jaws hungrily.

The lamb closed his eyes... and heard a shout. A stone went singing past his ear and the wolf was knocked to the ground. And there came David, striding up the hillside!

'Ouch!' cried the wolf. 'That hurt!' He took one

look at David, who was fitting another stone into his sling, and slunk away.

David lifted the lamb gently into his arms.

'What an exciting day it's been for you,' he said. 'For me as well. But we must both go home now.'

The lamb snuggled down with a contented sigh and listened drowsily to David singing as he made his way down the hillside.

'Even if I go through the deepest darkness, I will not be afraid, Lord, for you are with me. Your shepherd's rod and staff protect me.'

By the time they had reached the safety of the fields, the lamb was fast asleep.

9

The Lions' Revolt

Daniel and his friends were Jews who had studied in Babylon and now lived comfortable lives as advisers to the king. Although they were far from their homes in Jerusalem, they tried to follow God and keep his laws. Daniel had been given a special gift from God—he could understand and interpret dreams and strange signs. The king had made Daniel his chief adviser. But many people became jealous of Daniel, and plotted to kill him.

The lion's tail twitched as he paced up and down the pit which was his home.

'Have you heard the latest news?' he asked.

'I do wish you'd stop doing that,' said the second lion, yawning loudly. 'It's very tiring.'

'Doing what?'

'Pacing up and down.'

'I'm not interested in news,' grumbled the third lion, who had once been a large and handsome beast, but now looked worn and old. 'I'm more interested in our next meal. That last batch of humans was pretty tough. I've had stomach ache ever since and my fur has begun falling out.'

'That's because we don't get any fresh air,' explained the first lion, who was still pacing up and down. 'Stuck here in this dark pit day after day, expected to live on a diet of humans, humans and more humans, and most of them so thin there's no meat on them—why, it's enough to turn any self-respecting lion vegetarian! Is that a balanced diet, I ask? I'm only surprised we've lasted this long.'

'What do you propose to do about it?' asked the second lion with another yawn.

'Nothing,' said the first lion bitterly. 'There's nothing we can do. But you haven't heard my news.'

'Oh, go on then. I don't suppose we'll get any peace until you tell us.'

'Well,' said the first lion, 'King Darius's advisers are jealous of Daniel.'

'Who's Daniel?' asked the third lion.

'Daniel's the chief adviser to the king. He's a Jewish prophet, and the other advisers are terribly jealous because he's been put in charge over them. They keep trying to trick him into doing something wrong so that he can be punished. First they tried to prove that he was swindling the king, but they couldn't, for Daniel's a very honest man. So now they've thought up another plan. They've asked the king to make a law saying that for thirty days no one can ask anything from any god or any person other than from the king.'

'Has the king agreed?' asked the third lion.

'Oh, yes.'

'So what?' said the second lion. 'It doesn't mean we'll get better food or a nicer home, does it?'

The first lion sighed. 'What have I done to be stuck in a lion pit with two such stupid lions? Anyone who disobeys this law will be thrown to us! It'll mean food, lots and lots of food, you stupid great cats!'

'Why?' asked the second lion.

'It's such a ridiculous law, there're bound to be hundreds of people who'll break it!'

'You mean, if a man asks his friend to give him a bite of his lunch, that's against the law?' asked the third lion slowly.

'Yes.'

'Or if a wife asks her husband to take in the washing, that's against the law too?'

'Yes!'

'Well, I never,' said the second lion.

'King Darius won't have many subjects left,' said the third lion, beginning to grin. 'We'll have eaten them.'

'Why did the king agree to such a silly law?' asked the second lion.

'Because he was flattered by the idea.'

'He'll change it, once he finds out what it really means,' said the third lion.

'That's the beauty of it,' said the first lion. 'He can't! This kind of law can't be changed.'

'Just remind me—why did the king's advisers suggest it in the first place?' asked the second lion.

'As a means to trap Daniel,' said the first lion.

'Why?'

'Daniel spends a lot of his time praying to God and asking him for advice. If he carries on doing that over the next thirty days, he's in trouble.'

The third lion licked his lips. 'Is he tasty?' he asked. 'Is there much meat on him?'

'Just a minute,' said the second lion. 'Just hold on a minute. How do you know all this?'

'Because...' said the first lion, then stopped.

'Because...?'

'I said I wouldn't tell.'

'But we're your friends,' said the second lion. 'We share the same pit as you. You can't have secrets from us.'

'Well,' said the first lion slowly, 'he didn't exactly say not to tell you, I suppose. He just said that I should shut my mouth, so I thought he didn't want me to tell anyone.'

'We're not "anyone",' said the second lion.

'Oh, come on,' urged the third lion. 'Tell. I love secrets.'

The first lion made up his mind. 'All right then. It was last night. You were both asleep and snoring, as usual...'

'I don't snore!' said the second lion.

'Oh, yes, you do,' said the third lion.

'Suddenly the pit was filled with light and I saw this amazing creature with wings.'

'You must have been dreaming,' said the second lion.

'Or it might have been that old man you ate,' said the third. 'I thought he looked a bit green in the face when they threw him in.'

'It was an angel,' said the first lion. 'A messenger sent from God. And he told me just what I've told you.'

'Why did he tell you?' asked the third lion. 'Why not me? I'm older than you.'

The first lion shrugged. 'I expect God thought I was more intelligent.'

'What does the angel want us to do?' asked the second lion.

The first lion shook his head. 'I don't know.'

'So much for your intelligence!' snorted the third lion.

'Did the angel actually tell you to shut your mouth?' asked the second lion. 'It seems a funny thing to say.'

'No,' said the first lion, after some thought. 'He said that God would shut our mouths.'

'I think it could mean something completely different,' said the second lion slowly. 'I think it could mean that we shouldn't eat this Daniel, if he's thrown to us.'

'Then how are we going to stay alive?' wailed the third lion. 'I'm so hungry!'

'Perhaps God will help us if we do what he wants,' said the second lion.

'Yes,' said the first lion admiringly. 'That's really clever.' He became suddenly businesslike. 'That's decided then. As from now, we go on strike. We don't eat humans.'

'I never agreed to that,' said the third lion.

'Majority decision,' said the first lion briskly. 'All those in favour...?'

The second lion raised a paw.

'Carried.'

Just then the metal grill at the mouth of the pit opened. The face of a palace guard appeared.

'Pussy, pussy, pussy... hungry are we? We've a nice bit of juicy food for you all. Old Daniel, the king's chief adviser. Ex-chief adviser I should say. The king's not happy about it, but what can he do? Daniel asked God for advice and not the king. That's strictly against the rules. The law's the law. So here you are.'

And he thrust Daniel down into the lion's pit.

Daniel, a small, thin man, got to his feet and dusted down his robe. He looked at the lions, who were prowling round him, swallowed hard and began to pray.

'They look very fierce, God, and very hungry, and I'm scared of being eaten. I'm here because I've been loyal to you, God. I've got every faith in you and I know you love and care for me, so please… help me to be brave!'

'What's he saying?' asked the second lion.

'I think he must be praying to God,' said the first lion.

The lions stared at Daniel.

'Not much to write home about, is he?' said the first lion.

'Very bony,' agreed the second lion. 'Not a lot of meat.'

'No,' said the third lion regretfully, 'I suppose not.'

With that they turned their backs on Daniel, lay down and closed their eyes.

'Not that I'll get a wink of sleep,' grumbled the third lion. 'I'm so hungry, my stomach's rumbling.'

And Daniel, seeing that the lions were not going to eat him, thanked God, then he, too, lay down beside them and closed his eyes. But he did not get much sleep, either.

The following morning King Darius himself came to the entrance to the lion's pit and peered down.

'My poor Daniel,' said the king. 'My dear chief adviser. I've been so worried about you. I haven't slept a wink all night.'

'That makes four of us,' muttered the third lion. 'Five, if you include Daniel.'

Daniel got to his feet. 'May Your Majesty live for ever!'

The king was so amazed that he almost toppled over into the lion's pit.

'Why weren't you eaten?' he asked.

'I put my trust in God and the lions didn't hurt me,' said Daniel. 'God knew that I never wanted to harm you.'

The king was delighted.

'Pull him out!' he ordered his guards. And Daniel was pulled out of the pit.

'Huh,' said the third lion. 'He wasn't much, but he was food and now he's gone.'

But the king had not finished. 'Arrest the men who plotted against Daniel and throw them to the lions instead,' he ordered.

So the lions got their food after all.

'Still no exercise,' grumbled the first lion. 'Still stuck in this pit in the dark.'

'But with lots to eat,' said the third lion, a happy smile on his face.

10

The Whale's Worst Meal

Jonah was a prophet who disobeyed God. God wanted him to tell the people of the city of Nineveh that they must stop being wicked—if they did, God would forgive them. But Jonah didn't want God to forgive them. The people of Nineveh were from Assyria—they were Israel's arch enemies! So he ran away. But he soon found out that it's hard to run away from God...

'So you see,' said the whale, swimming up and down in front of the school of young dolphins, whales and porpoises, 'we are the most important creatures in the ocean. And why is that?' Flippers shot up.

'Because we're mammals,' said one of the dolphins.

'Precisely,' said the whale. 'We are mammals. We are warm-blooded. We have lungs. We breathe air. We are unique. We are not, and I repeat this, not fish.'

The class nodded obediently.

'So don't let me catch you mixing with those fish,' said the whale. 'They're common and stupid and only fit to be eaten.'

One of the dolphins raised a flipper. 'But my best friend, the weedy seadragon says...'

'I don't want to hear what your best friend says,' the whale interrupted sharply. 'God chose us to be his special creatures of the sea, and you shouldn't be hobnobbing with weedy seadragons, sea urchins or any other sea creatures. Now,' he said, in a less stern voice, 'to end our lessons today, I'll tell you about the adventure I had some years ago when I fought with a giant squid...'

The young dolphins, whales and porpoises sighed and looked longingly at the sun sparkling on the waves.

When school was over, the whale swam slowly out to sea. He was tired. Teaching was hard work. Night fell and, one by one, the stars came out. The whale drifted along, calmed by the gentle swell of the waters...

An enormous wave hit the whale, and he was lifted high on its surging crest. A storm had blown up out of nowhere. The wind howled and torrential rain blotted out the stars. The sea boiled and foamed. A ship appeared and the whale could see it being tossed like a toy, up and down the massive waves.

There were anguished cries from those on board.

The whale swam closer... and suddenly he gulped and swallowed. He could feel something large travelling down his throat and into his stomach. Something large and totally indigestible. Whatever could it be?

As quickly as it had blown up, the storm died down. The sea grew calm and the ship sailed away.

Then the whale heard a voice. It was an odd sort of voice, small and echoey.

'Oh, God!' it cried.

The whale looked around. The ocean was empty.

'Oh, God!' the voice cried again.

'Who are you?' asked the whale.

'Jonah,' said the voice.

The whale looked round once more.

'What are you?' he asked. 'A fish?'

'I'm a man,' said the voice.

The whale looked round again. He could see no sign of a man swimming in the water.

'Where are you?' he asked.

'In your stomach.'

'Whatever are you doing there?'

'You swallowed me.'

The whale was silent for a moment.

'Are you sure?' he asked at last.

'Quite sure.'

'You mean, I swallowed you whole?'

'Yes.'

'Arms, legs and all the bits?'

'Yes.'

'And I thought it was indigestion,' said the whale. Jonah began to cry. 'It's all my fault,' he sobbed.

'Why's that?' asked the whale. 'And do try not to cry. It's making my insides feel very squelchy.'

'God told me to take a message to the people living in the city of Nineveh,' Jonah sniffled. 'They're very bad people. God told me to tell them that unless they were sorry for being so evil and promised to turn over a new leaf, he would punish them. But I didn't want to go.'

'Why?' asked the whale.

'I was ready to preach to my people, the Israelites, but I didn't see why I should go and preach to a load of foreigners,' said Jonah. 'You might not know it but we are God's chosen ones, the most important people in the entire world.'

'Rather like us whales,' the whale said, understandingly.

'And as far as I'm concerned, those people of Nineveh have only themselves to blame for being so wicked. I think they deserve every punishment they get.'

'I see,' said the whale.

'So I decided to run away,' said Jonah.

'Run away?'

'Yes. I thought if I got on a ship and sailed for Tarshish, I'd be out of God's reach.'

'But you landed up in my stomach instead,' said the whale.

'Yes,' said Jonah. 'It's not that easy to run away from God.'

'I feel sick,' said the whale.

'I don't feel very well myself,' said Jonah.

'So what happens now?' asked the whale. 'I mean, I'm just a teacher so I'm not exactly used to this sort of thing.'

'You think I am?' said Jonah.

The whale swam on in silence.

'Where are we going?' asked Jonah.

'I don't know,' said the whale.

Jonah sniffled.

'Now don't start to cry again,' said the whale anxiously.

'If only God would forgive me, I'll do anything he wants,' Jonah wailed. 'I'll even go to Nineveh, if only he'll save me.'

'But I've already saved you,' the whale objected. 'Do get your facts right. I was the one who saved you from drowning. I do dislike muddled thinking.'

Jonah wasn't listening. He was praying to God. For the rest of that night and for all the following day, he prayed to God. The whale grew quite tired of it.

'Do you have to pray so loudly?' he asked. 'You

can't think how uncomfortable it is to have one's stomach praying all the time. It's making me feel quite unwell.'

'I'm sorry,' said Jonah. 'It's all my fault.'

'I know it is,' said the whale crossly.

For two more days and nights the whale swam across the ocean with Jonah praying in his stomach. On the fourth morning the whale, tired from his journey and hungry from not having eaten sighted land. He swam slowly towards it and flopped onto the beach. There he was violently sick. A thin, white-faced Jonah crawled out.

'So that's what you look like,' said the whale looking him over. 'A pretty miserable specimen if I might say.'

Jonah had fallen to his knees and was praying loudly.

'I'll go to Nineveh, God,' he said. 'I'll go anywhere. Thank you for saving me.'

With that, he ran off.

'It would be nice if I got some thanks, too,' called the whale after him, but Jonah was out of earshot.

The whale had to rest before he felt strong enough to return to his school, far out in the ocean. But just as he was about to swim away, he saw Jonah walking slowly along the beach towards him. There was a big smile on the man's face and he was rubbing his hands together gleefully.

'If you're thinking you'll stow away again, you're

very mistaken!' said the whale and closed his mouth firmly.

Jonah shuddered. 'No thank you. I've come to watch the fun.'

'Fun?' asked the whale.

'Fire,' said Jonah hopefully. 'Brimstone. Perhaps both.'

'What do you mean?'

'I'm expecting God to destroy the city and it should be quite spectacular. I thought I'd come back here to watch.'

'Wouldn't the people listen to you?' asked the whale.

'Oh, they listened all right,' said Jonah. 'They all said they were sorry they'd offended God and promised not to be wicked again. Even their king said he was sorry.'

'So that's all right then,' said the whale.

Jonah shrugged. 'I suppose so, but I'm still hoping that God will wipe them out. They don't really deserve to live, do they?'

'I don't know about that,' said the whale. 'You told me that God said he would punish them if they didn't turn from their wicked ways. Now you tell me that they have turned from their wicked ways—so what reason has God to destroy their city? There's no logic in it.'

Jonah shrugged again. 'Who needs logic?' he said. 'And who needs excuses? God certainly doesn't. Why don't you stay and watch?' He wiped his brow. 'Phew, it's hot, isn't it?' he said, and settled himself comfortably on the ground under the shade of a large plant.

The following morning, the sun rose, hotter than ever. The city of Nineveh was still standing, but the plant which had provided shade for Jonah was dead.

Jonah was furious. He jumped up and down, and shook his fist at the sky. The whale watched with interest.

'Why did you make the plant die and not destroy Nineveh, God?' he shouted. 'I don't think that's very fair of you!'

'Jonah,' God said gently, 'you are angry because the plant you were sitting under died. You did not create that plant and did nothing to save it. I created it and chose not to save it to teach you a lesson. You are also angry because you want the people of Nineveh to die. But I also created all the people who live in the city of Nineveh. You want its people destroyed, for you look down on them because they are different. But they have as much right to my mercy and my forgiveness as you. They are as important to me as you.'

Jonah fell on the ground and burst into tears. The whale looked at him thoughtfully for a while, then quietly swam away.

The dolphins, whales and porpoises had all been

having a wonderful holiday while their teacher was gone and were not at all happy at the whale's return a few days later.

'Now listen to me, all of you,' said the whale sternly, when he managed to get them back in line. He blew loudly through his air hole. 'I have something of great importance to tell you. It goes against the grain to say this but we are not the most important creatures in the entire ocean. We may be unique, but so are all God's creatures and he cares for all of us, from the humblest tiddler to the largest shark.'

The young dolphins, whales and porpoises looked at him in astonishment.

'Now,' said the whale briskly, 'to finish school for today, I'll tell you how I came to learn this amazing fact. It all began with a great storm...'

His class sighed and looked longingly at the inviting blue waters of the sea.